# My Friend with Autism

Written By: Beverly Bishop        Illustrated By: Craig Bishop

**FUTURE HORIZONS** INC.

721 W. Abram Street, Arlington, Texas 76013
817-277-0727
800-489-0727
817-277-2270 (Fax)
E-mail: info@futurehorizons-autism.com
www.FutureHorizons-autism.com

Cataloging in Publication Data is available from the Library of Congress.
ISBN 1-885477-89-9

This book is dedicated to the Lord God who has taught me to be thankful for autism, to Seth who has shown me the joy in autism, and to Thad and Breanne who are the best dad and sister Seth could ever want.

Many thanks to Angela Telfer who is changing the world, one autistic child at a time and to Bruce Mills, without whom this book would be incomplete.

Thanks also to my Mom and Dad who have supported our family on this journey and have proofread and edited this book relentlessly.

## Introduction and Instructions for Adults

Welcome to *My Friend with Autism.* I designed this book for anyone who is being introduced to autism. Babysitters, friends, church members, neighbors, and anyone who comes into contact with an autistic child will find it both useful and entertaining. However, the book was written especially for young classmates, students, and parents of children with autism. The book explains, in a positive and understandable way, what autism is and how the behavior of autistic children can be different from that of typical children. Teachers can use this book in the classroom then send a copy home with each student so that parents can use it at home. I believe that parents will find the "Notes for Adults" section useful and thought provoking as it provides further information relating to each autistic trait mentioned in the children's section.

Teachers who have autistic spectrum children in their classrooms will find this book invaluable in helping to integrate autistic students into the typical student group. By helping the typical children understand the traits and behaviors of their autistic classmates, *My Friend with Autism* will encourage positive relationships and help to grow meaningful friendships among typical and autistic peers.

Parents are extremely important to the academic and social success of their child. Mom and Dad's interest in a child's behavior and education is one of the most important aspects in ensuring a child's success. This is why I designed this book to be taken home and read by parents. As parents read this book with their children, it will reinforce the child's classroom learning, and it will reassure parents that autistic students are indeed extraordinary and present an exceptional opportunity for learning and interaction.

While all the pictures in this book are intended to be colored, I realize that creative little minds (autistic or not) frequently like to draw their own pictures. Therefore, I have included blank pages at the end of the book for busy, imaginative young hands to use in creating their own masterpieces while teachers explain any additional unique characteristics of a specific autistic student in their classroom.

Every young mind—whether we call it typical or autistic—is different. Each is good at some things, and each has difficulty with other things. What is most important is remembering that each mind—each child—is special. All children have the potential to contribute great and important things to the world.

Beverly Bishop

June 2002

I have a friend with autism.  He is good at many things.

My friend's ears work really well. He can hear sounds I may not even hear. He is almost always the first one to hear an airplane or a train coming. This is why he sometimes covers his ears even when things don't seem loud to me.

My friend's eyes work really well.  He sees little things that I might not even notice.  His eyes work so well that bright lights or a sunny day will often hurt his eyes.

My friend's sense of taste works really well.  He can taste even a little bit of pepper in his food.  This is why he only eats certain foods, and why he sometimes doesn't want foods that are too hot or cold.

My friend has a strong sense of touch.  He can feel even the smallest little thing touching him.  This makes him very ticklish, and sometimes he doesn't like to be touched. Other times, his sense of touch makes him want to touch me.  If I don't want him to touch me, I ask him nicely not to touch me.

My friend is very strong.  Sometimes he forgets how strong he is, and he gives hugs that are too hard.  Sometimes he just plays too roughly with me.  I can help him by reminding him to be gentle and by remembering not to play too roughly myself.

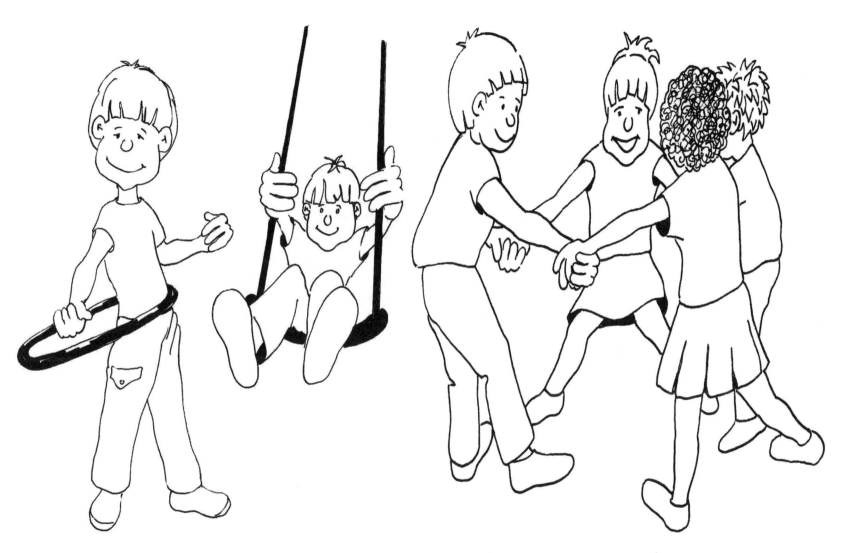

I can help my friend by playing games with lots of moving, running, dancing, or swinging.  When I play with my friend, I do not have to worry that I will get autism because autism cannot be caught like a cold or the flu.

My friend is very smart.  He is good at counting, the alphabet, and at many other things. He knew the letters of the alphabet even when he was a little boy.  My friend likes it when I play with letters and numbers with him, maybe even spelling or counting.

Just like me, my friend is good at playing. He especially loves to play with cars, trucks, trains, and things that spin. Sometimes he plays differently than I do, but I can help him by watching the way he plays and then trying what he is doing right next to him. Then maybe sometime he will try doing what I like to do.

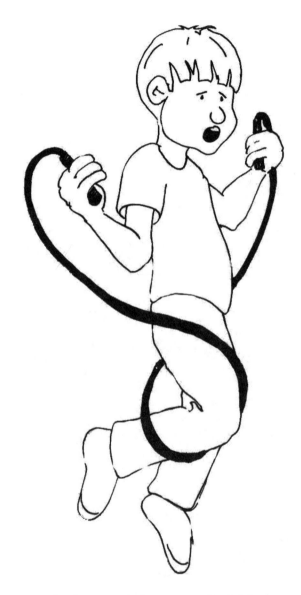

My friend with autism is good at many things.  But his autism also makes some things hard for him.

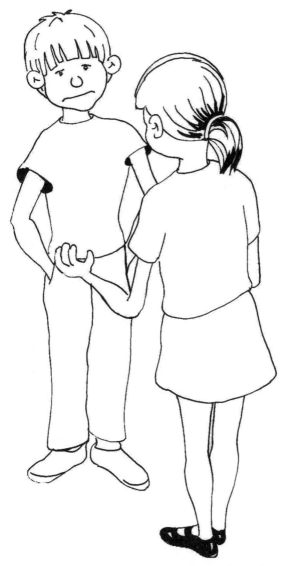

Talking is sometimes hard for my friend. But when he doesn't talk, my feelings are not hurt because I understand that talking is hard for him. Sometimes I can even help him by suggesting some words he might want to say.

My friend may still want to play with me even if he doesn't talk much.  Sometimes it helps him when I just keep playing and talking with him, even if he doesn't talk or if his words don't make sense to me.

Understanding other people's feelings is hard for my friend. He does not always understand that I have feelings too. When I see a person crying, I know that the person is probably sad. But when my friend sees a person crying, he may not understand what it means.

Sharing is hard for my friend. He doesn't understand how much fun it can be to share his toys or that my feelings are hurt when he takes toys away from me. I still ask my friend to share with me, but if he says no or if he does not answer at a time when he really should be sharing, I usually ask an adult for help.

Change is often very hard for my friend. Sometimes when he is doing one thing and it is time to start doing something different, he gets frustrated. I can help him with this by telling him what is going to happen next. For example, just before recess, I might remind him that in a few more minutes it will be time to go outside.

Sitting still and quiet is hard for my friend. When it is time to sit quietly, I can help him by showing him how well I sit quietly. Sometimes I can also help by reminding him to use a quiet voice.

Ff  G8  Hh  Ii  Jj  Kĸ  LI  Mm

PLAY OUTSIDE    COMPUTER    LIBRARY

Because some things are hard for my friend, adults may use pictures to help him understand better.  I like seeing his pictures and learning what they mean.  Sometimes I can use his pictures to help him with things like sharing, changing activities, or understanding feelings.

Just like me, my friend does many things very well and some other things are hard for him.  Most of all, my friend loves to have friends.

# NOTES FOR ADULTS

The purpose of this section is to provide adults with a more detailed explanation of each page in the children's portion of this book. It also includes ideas for adults to use when helping with an autistic child. This is not an exhaustive or scientific discussion of autism. Instead, it is intended to be a helpful tool to be shared with friends, family, Sunday school teachers, the parents of peers, or other adults who come into contact with an autistic child. The goal is to give enough understanding for an adult to guide typical children into meaningful relationships with an autistic child. It will also help to reduce any fear adults working with an autistic child may have.

Please note that because 75% of children with autism are male, masculine pronouns are used in order to avoid the clumsiness of him/her. This is not intended to ignore the many wonderful girls who have autism.

### Page 1 - What is autism?

Autism is a neurological disorder that may affect more than 1 child in every 500 children. Children may either be born with autism or develop it within the first few years of life. The cause of autism is currently unknown, and there is currently no cure for autism. However, many strategies and treatments may be used very successfully to help the autistic child.

Autism affects the way the brain interprets and communicates information. One of the most common effects of autism is the brain's inconsistency in interpreting information received from the senses (sight, taste, smell, touch and hearing). Each sense can be either over-sensitive or under-sensitive, and the level of sensitivity of each sense may actually change daily or throughout a day. A good way of understanding it is that the connection between the senses and the brain seem to have short circuits—sometimes they work and sometimes they don't.

Although the five senses listed above are the most well-known senses, the human central nervous system is actually comprised of many more senses than just these five. Two other senses that are often affected are the vestibular sense and the proprioceptive sense. The vestibular sense is the body's sense of movement and the proprioceptive sense is the body's internal sense of position in space. Many people have experienced confusion from these internal senses when on strong pain medication or while recovering from anesthesia. It's hard to imagine experiencing such confusion most of the time! Although these senses are often extremely troubling for autistic children, they are not covered in this book because it is difficult to present these concepts to young children. However, more information can be learned about these senses by reading about "Sensory Integration Dysfunction."

Autism is called a spectrum disorder because the degree to which a person is affected can vary greatly. The traits of two autistic people may be completely different. The spectrum ranges from children who are considered aloof (usually unable to speak and seemingly separated from the world) to high-functioning (usually speaking well and able to function with peers). Asperger's Syndrome is another term that is sometimes used to describe high-functioning people within the autistic spectrum. The behaviors described are typical of children with high-functioning autism or Asperger's syndrome; however, it is important to remember that every child with autism is unique. Some of the traits in this book may exactly match another child with autism, while other traits are completely different for the same child. These variations do not make a child "more or less autistic," instead these variations make every child with autism one-of-a-kind, just like every other child.

### Page 2 - Hearing

The brain of a person with autism may misinterpret sounds. Many autistic adults have described their hearing as having no background noise. In other words, everything they hear comes in at the same volume level. Imagine hearing the person who is talking to you, the refrigerator fan, the people in the room having other conversations, and the airplane flying over outside all at the same volume level. It would be difficult to sort the important sound from the unimportant. What would seem a "normal" or even an unnoticeable amount of background noise to a nonautistic listener may be overwhelming or unbearable to the autistic listener.

Some sounds may actually cause physical pain to the autistic listener. Sometimes these sounds are loud, but often they are just everyday sounds that most people do not even notice. Particular sounds that others may consider normal or unnoticeable may also cause fear for an autistic child. To an autistic child ordinary sounds may be scary if they are sudden or unpredictable.

Adults can help an autistic child with this by trying to help the child focus on what is important, making sure that the child is paying attention before speaking, and by talking directly to the child. Busy or noisy environments can be very overwhelming to an autistic child because everything seems so loud. A sudden temper tantrum or other negative behavior can often be caused by too much noise or by a particular noise that disturbs the child. It sometimes takes detective work to discover exactly what is upsetting an autistic child, and sometimes it can never be understood.

When in loud or busy places, it may be useful to allow autistic children to take breaks in quiet places. Remember, autistic children are trying to communicate through behavior. As adults, we must try to figure out what the child is attempting to communicate, and respond appropriately. Warning an autistic child of an upcoming sound may also be very helpful (fire drills, whistles, vacuum cleaners, drills, mixers, etc.) so that the sound is not unexpected.

## Page 3 - Vision

The visual senses of an autistic person can also be both over-sensitive or under-sensitive. Therefore, an autistic child may see things others cannot see, such as light patterns or the individual specks of color that make up a picture. Imagine trying to view an entire room through a telescope or a tube. By doing this, details of specific objects would be more obvious, but how the objects fit together in the room would be difficult to figure out. This may be how autistic people view what is around them. What they do see may be in great detail, but they may not be able to see the whole picture very well. Some autistic children may even feel physical pain or possibly not be able to see at all when lights are too bright. Many autistic children also have difficulty making eye contact. This may be an autistic child's way of minimizing visual stimulation or it may be caused by a connection that simply isn't working in the brain.

Suggesting a baseball cap or sunglasses before going outside in bright sunlight is one thing that adults could try to help an autistic child who has over-sensitive vision. Adults should also remember that a child's closing his eyes, putting his head down, or intentionally staring at a wall or off into space, may be ways that the autistic child communicates that he is being overwhelmed visually. Also, remember that an autistic child may be listening and indeed paying very close attention to you even if he is not making any eye contact at all.

## Page 4 - Taste

Many autistic children are very picky eaters. Some children have a diet consisting of less than ten foods. The sensation of hot or cold in an autistic child's mouth may be painful. For example, the taste of ice cream may be pleasing, but the coldness is painful. If the child is willing to force the ice cream down, he may have a distressed look or may even run around in circles.

Adults can help in this area by understanding that eating is also related to the senses of sight, touch, and smell. Some textures or smells may be offensive or even painful to an autistic child, causing them to not even be willing to taste a particular food.

Some autistic children find that the sense of touch in their mouth is more sensitive than touching with their hands. This may entice the child to put something in his mouth in order to try to feel it or in order to get some sensory stimulation from it. This may be why an autistic child will try licking or even eating unusual objects like bricks, reflectors, or sand.

Adults can help by watching carefully to make sure an autistic child doesn't ingest harmful things and by trying to minimize any ridiculing from peers when this occurs. Firmly telling the autistic child "no" and trying to redirect his attention is often the best solution. If this is a common problem, parents or teachers might use a repetitive phrase in order to help. For example, consistently saying, "not in your mouth, this is not food." Sometimes helping an autistic child's peers to memorize a phrase to say when they see their autistic friend putting things in his mouth will cause the peers to feel helpful and will reduce ridicule because it gives the peers something else to do besides tease.

## Page 5 – Touch

For many autistic children, touch seems to be the sense that swings the most between over-reactive and under-reactive. Within a few hours, touch sensitivity may swing from high to low. Some autistic people have said that a simple touch on the arm can sometimes feel like they have received a shot. For many autistic children, any touch that is unexpected is uncomfortable. An autistic child may have trouble standing in lines because of his fear that someone behind him might touch him.

Adults should remember that a pat on the head may not be positive for an autistic child, instead it may be distressing. For some children, sitting in the back of a room full of children or standing at the back of the line may be much easier because they do not have to be as fearful of an unexpected touch. When children line up, sitting rather than standing often eliminates pushing, touching, and other troublesome behaviors. Adults can also remember that a firm touch is often easier for an autistic child to handle than a light stroking motion.

An autistic child may crave deep pressure when his sense of touch is overwhelmed. Many autistic children will crawl under rugs, carpets, couch cushions, blankets, or anything else that will give them a sense of even pressure. The child may be trying to communicate that his sense of touch is out of balance, and an adult may be able to help by finding ways for the child to get firm, even pressure on his body.

## Page 6 – Strength

An autistic child may seem unable to be gentle with things or people. This may be a result of an under-sensitive sense of touch. This may also result from hyperactivity in many autistic children. Regardless of the cause, many autistic children are described as rough and full of energy.

Adults can help by trying to determine the motive of an aggressive behavior so that a better alternative may be taught for whatever the child is trying to communicate. For example, an autistic child may hit in order to show affection. Instead of simply disciplining for hitting, it would also help to teach that a hug would be more appropriate. Allowing plenty of time for exercise and teaching the appropriate places and times to burn off this energy often helps as well. Certain activities, such as swinging, spinning, or jumping, are often very effective.

Adults can also help by realizing that an autistic child's boundless energy is also often coupled with a lack of fear. This may put the autistic child at risk of danger to himself or others if the child is not supervised closely. For instance, an autistic child may suddenly run across a busy street or ride his bike down a steep hill without realizing the danger.

## Page 7 – Pretending

An autistic child often does not understand abstract concepts or pretend play. This may make it difficult for the child to join in to many childhood games which require pretending. One of the biggest challenges can be when children play roughly (wrestling, boxing, kick-boxing, etc.). An autistic child may be unable to discriminate between a pretend punch and a real punch. Therefore, when the autistic child does try to join in with the other children, he may hurt someone. Adults should supervise very closely if this kind of play is allowed at all.

## Page 8 - Intelligence

The term savant has been used to describe autistic people who have an unusual intellectual ability in one particular area. The most common areas are math, arts, and memory, although an autistic child may excel in any area. Many autistic children learn counting and the alphabet very young, some even before they can talk. Some autistic children have amazing memories for facts or physical locations.

A child does not have to be a savant in any area in order to be autistic. Many children do not excel more than typical peers in any academic or artistic area.

Adults can help with this by remembering to praise the autistic child for his strengths. Autistic children sometimes receive so much correction that it is very important to search for areas to reinforce the positive. It also helps with peer relationships if adults praise the student in front of his peers. Working with an autistic child in his area of strength may also have a very calming effect upon the child. For example, if a child who loves the alphabet is distressed about a noisy, crowded classroom, sitting with the child to write letters on paper or sing the ABC's might help. Remembering to use a current strength or interest in order to teach a new skill can also be very helpful.

## Page 9 - Playing

Many autistic children go through stages of being obsessed with particular toys or subjects. The transportation industry is one of the most common obsessions for high-functioning autistic children, although this is not true for all autistic children. Autistic children may be found lining up their toys in straight lines, watching toys spin, or disassembling and reassembling toys rather than playing with toys as typical peers might.

Adults can help by realizing that many autistic children want desperately to have friends and to "fit in" with their peers but cannot make sense out of their peers' actions. One way for adults to encourage friendships is to urge the peer to try doing what the autistic child is doing. Sometimes after a connection has been made this way, the autistic child will then try to do what the peer wants to do. However, adults should remember that meaningful social relationships do not often come quickly or easily. Adults and peers must be very persistent and may need to assist with many different strategies before any connections are made.

## Pages 11 & 12 – Talking

Language is a very individualized area for autistic children. Some autistic children never talk, others begin talking very late. Some use only memorized phrases or scripts, and others have excellent language skills, but tend to have mostly one-sided conversations or seem to lack understanding.

Adults can help by assisting peers in finding ways to communicate with the autistic child. Help peers to know that they are not necessarily being ignored. Continue encouraging peers to talk with an autistic child. If the child has the ability to talk, but doesn't respond, an adult might tell the autistic child what an appropriate answer to a peer's question would be. The language of many autistic children is composed of phrases they have memorized or recently heard. Often these phrases or scripts are from television, movies, videos, or overheard conversations. Adults should also understand that inappropriate phrases, which are blurted out with no understandable context, might be triggered by a word or sound that the child heard or may be a way the child comforts himself. Many autistic children will continually mumble or quote long, memorized scripts. Adults can also help by carefully monitoring what an autistic child hears, as it can be very difficult to train an autistic child to stop saying a memorized phrase that is inappropriate.

## Page 13 – Feelings

Emotions are typically very difficult for autistic children. Often autistic children cannot read body language or facial expression as other children can. As well as not understanding other people's emotions, autistic children often struggle with their own emotions. Negative behavior can sometimes occur because an autistic child is feeling an emotion that is simply overwhelming or that he cannot figure out how to communicate.

Adults can help by identifying the autistic child's emotions and the emotions of other people. Naming the emotion and coming up with an appropriate way to express it can be very helpful. Often, an autistic child's behavior is a way to communicate emotions for which he cannot find words. Often, a task that is normally simple for an autistic child will become virtually impossible when he is experiencing an emotion.

**Page 14 - Sharing**

Sharing is difficult for all children. But, it is especially difficult to teach when an autistic child struggles with the ability to see something from another person's perspective. Autistic children most often lack the ability to empathize. They may believe that we are all thinking the same thoughts or have only one mind rather than that we all have unique thoughts and beliefs.

Adults can help by giving the autistic child something concrete to help him understand when and with whom to share. Statements such as "two more minutes until your turn" are often effective when sharing is needed. Sometimes, redirecting the child to another activity will work. Taking turns with two people or continuing around a circle are very concrete, and autistic children sometimes do well with these once learned. Again, remember that teaching sharing is a long process for all children and requires patience and endurance.

**Page 15 – Change**

Autistic children feel a strong need for structure. They need to understand what the rules are and exactly how things are going to happen. Autistic children may struggle when they expect things to happen one way, but they happen another way. They may get upset if a schedule changes or something is different from normal.

Adults can help with this by reminding them of what is going to happen next or explaining in advance when a change is going to happen. Often, pictures or icons are very calming for autistic children and help them understand the order of events. It is also easy to rearrange the pictures to show a child that a change is going to take place. Adults can also help by making transitions from one activity to another as smooth as possible. For instance, in a classroom setting, if the children get out of control for a few moments while the teacher is switching from one activity to another, other children may be very easy to calm and redirect for the next activity. But, the autistic child will be very frustrated by this quick change. It is much easier for an autistic child if the moments in the middle are eliminated and they move directly from the first activity to the second.

**Page 16 – Quiet Times**

Many autistic children are capable of sitting quietly, but will choose not to unless the issue is pushed. It is important to find out from parents or teachers how long an autistic child can reasonably be expected to sit quietly.

Adults should be sure of what is reasonable and should then make sure that the autistic child understands what is expected and what the consequences are for not sitting quietly. Then, adults need to be very consistent with the enforcement of these consequences, as consistency will help the autistic child to be successful. Creating something concrete to demonstrate how long quiet time will last may also be helpful. For instance, something that is moved along a line from start to finish as the quiet time continues may be helpful. Sometimes giving a concrete signal that the child can watch for when the quiet time is done will help him wait quietly watching for the signal.

**Page 17 - Pictures**

Autistic children often benefit greatly from pictures or icons that they can see and associate with certain activities or words. Pictures can often be used to express feelings before words can be used. If an autistic child is able to choose activities or objects, pictures may assist the child in making these decisions. Verbal instructions regarding choices can be overwhelming to the autistic child. For example, if the child can choose between juice, water, or milk, show the child all three options and then let him choose. Icons representing various play activities can also be helpful.

Adults can help peers by finding ways to make pictures and icons fun for everyone. Adults can also effectively use pictures to communicate consequences to actions by saying and showing that if this picture happens, then this picture will happen, or more simply, first this, then this.

**Page 18 – Conclusion**

In summary, it is important for adults to remember that an autistic child's reaction to over-responsive or under-responsive senses can vary from complete shut-down to extreme emotional outbursts. The child's response is often driven by the natural "fight or flight" response. As adults we must be constantly studying and evaluating situations in order to try to understand what an autistic child is trying to communicate through his behavior.

It is also important that all of this information not be used to excuse inappropriate behavior by an autistic child. The goal is to train the child to behave appropriately. However, understanding the possible causes for behavior is the first step toward positive change.

Most high-functioning autistic children or children with Asperger's Syndrome do desire to have friends, but often find it difficult to understand and relate to their peers. An adult will find it very rewarding when a way is found to help an autistic child establish a meaningful relationship with a peer.

## Behaviors which may be Suggestive of an Autistic Spectrum Disorder

Delayed, little, or no speech OR sophisticated, adult-like speech

Speech patterns which frequently echo other people's exact words

Absence of nonverbal communication, such as pointing, gesturing, or even taking an adult's hand and leading him or her to something

Sometimes seems to not hear or understand simple directions

Lack of eye contact or difficulty making eye contact with others

Difficulty playing with peers (doesn't join in or seem to understand the pretend play of others)

Unusual or strange methods of playing with toys (repeatedly lining things up or twirling them)

Hands cover ears at unexpected sounds (indicating pain or fear)

Walking on tiptoes consistently when shoes are removed

Extreme temper tantrums when a routine is disrupted (took a different route to go to the store)

Reversed pronouns ("You want a cookie please" —meaning "I want a cookie")

Seems unaware of the feelings of others (no reaction to someone getting hurt or someone crying)

# Ten Quick Strategies for Helping an Autistic Child

**1. Simplify your language**, especially when the child is frustrated. Say, "Come here, please." instead of saying, "Mommy wants you to come here and stay close to me, so you will be safe when we are walking in the parking lot." Hand gestures may also be helpful.

**2. Give the child ways to cope with sensory problems.** For example, if the child is over-stimulated by sound, let the child wear earplugs or headphones when needed. It is important to balance stimulating, social activities with quiet, non-social times. Remember that people with autism spectrum disorders "fill up quickly" with social events. Determine the calming sensory experiences for your child (deep pressure, squeeze hugs, lights off) and be sure to incorporate them into daily activities. This will help the child regroup and will calm his heightened nervous system

**3. If the child can read, use written words to communicate during stressful situations.** For example, if the child is in the grocery store, and he is upset because the Pop-tarts are not in their usual place, write on a piece of paper: " It is okay. We can ask for help. Maybe there are more Pop-tarts in the back. If not, we can get them at a different store when we leave."

**4. Give the child a visual and an oral schedule** of daily activities. Use pictures, written words, or objects to communicate what is coming next. The child may then cross off each activity when it is finished. A posted daily schedule can provide comfort and security to the child. Perhaps the biggest advantage of using a visual schedule is that it gives an effective way to communicate that a change is going to happen before it actually happens.

**5. Use a calendar to show special events**, trips, or vacations. Use pictures or written words to make those events clear. The child can cross off each day of the week to get a visual picture of how close the special event is getting.

**6. Use the "First—Then" strategy.** Using pictures or words, communicate to the child, "First brush your teeth, then watch a video. First teeth, then video."

**7. Use the phrase, "The rule is_____"** when you can teach the child a social rule. Be sure to tell the child the reason for that rule.

**8. Purposefully, catch the child doing the right thing** and then praise his action specifically. It is often very effective to include words like, "What a smart thing to do." Autistic children often pride themselves on intelligence.

**9. Be consistent.** The more calm and consistent you can be, the "safer" the child will feel. Kids like to know that "whenever I do this, that happens." This doesn't mean that you need to be harsh, just stick to rules and expectations that you have established.

**10. Give the child choices.** Provide pictures or written choices for your child (chicken or cheeseburger? Play outside or playdoh?) If your child has trouble making choices, help him pick one of two choices and follow through with it. After some guided practice, he will likely make an independent choice.

**A PARENT'S GUIDE TO AUTISM** (Charles A. Hart, 1993)

This reassuring book provides answers to the many initial questions parents may have. The question and answer format makes it easy to read and understand.

**THE OUT OF SYNC CHILD: RECOGNIZING AND MAKING SENSE OF SENSORY INTEGRATION DYSFUNCTION** (Carol Stock Kranowitz, 1998-paperback)

Sensory integration dysfunction can be confusing. Carol Kranowitz is able to describe it in terms which make it much less confusing. This book teaches how to identify sensory integration issues and provides coping strategies that can soften sensory difficulties.

**BUILDING BRIDGES THROUGH SENSORY INTEGRATION** (Aquilla, Sutton, Yack 1998)

This book, written by an occupational therapist, contains sensory processing activities and strategies for home, school, and child care settings. It also provides strategies for challenging behaviors. An easy-to-read, 186-page manual.

**CHILDREN WITH AUTISM, A PARENTS' GUIDE** (Michael Powers, Editor, 1989)

A comprehensive guide. The quotes from parents' personal experiences add valuable insight and perspective. This book is a reference that will be used over and over again.

**THE NEW SOCIAL STORIES BOOK: ILLUSTRATED EDITION** (Carol Gray, 2000)

Social stories are a great way to help children understand social rules. This book is full of examples and explains how to write your own social stories.

**VISUAL STRATEGIES FOR IMPROVING COMMUNICATION: PRACTICAL SUPPORTS FOR SCHOOL AND HOME** (Linda Hodgdon, 1995)

This book is a wonderful resource that is easily used by parents, teachers and speech and language therapists. It is full of great ideas with specific examples!

**SOLVING BEHAVIOR PROBLEMS IN AUTISM: IMPROVING COMMUNICATION WITH VISUAL STRATEGIES** (Linda Hodgdon, 1999)

Linda Hodgdon demonstrates how the use of visual strategies can decrease behavior problems. Linda provides numerous examples to use as a guide.

**EMERGENCE - LABELED AUTISTIC** (Grandin & Scariano) Reprint in 1996.

A must read for those who wish to gain an insider's view of autism. In telling us the story of her "emergence" from autism, Temple Grandin offers invaluable insights into what it means to grow up with autism and thus how "typical" or non-autistic individuals might better understand and respond to the impairment.

**THINKING IN PICTURES** (Temple Grandin, 1995)

In this book, Grandin offers a collection of essays that address key dimensions of autism (e.g., diagnosis, sensory issues, relationships). While still drawing from personal experiences, the book approaches autism from a more scientific perspective.

**ASPERGER'S SYNDROME: A GUIDE FOR PARENTS AND PROFESSIONALS** (Tony Attwood, 1998)

Tony's book covers it all. In this leading resource in the field of Asperger Syndrome, Attwood describes the characteristics of Asperger's Syndrome in detail and offers strategies to teach about emotions, social skills, language, sensory issues, and more.

**PRETENDING TO BE NORMAL: LIVING WITH ASPERGER'S SYNDROME** (Liane Holliday Willey, 1999)

Liane's book provides an inside perspective of how people with Asperger's Syndrome view the world. Liane's message is one we all need to hear: value individual differences—these differences make the world a richer place.

## THE ILLUSTRATOR

### Craig Bishop

Craig Bishop worked as an art educator in Michigan Public Schools for thirty years. He retired from Western Michigan University in Kalamazoo, Michigan, as an instructor in Art Education, where he also received his early training in art.

He continues to paint, illustrate and do a monthly cartoon for Encore magazine. He also teaches painting at the Art Center of Battle Creek. Craig and his wife Jan live in Battle Creek, Michigan and enjoy being grandparents to Henry and Lucy.